Dead on Town Line

Dead

ON

Town Line

by Leslie Connor

illustrations by

Gina Triplett

Dial Books

DIAL BOOKS
A member of Penguin Group (USA) Inc.
Published by The Penguin Group
Penguin Group (USA) Inc., 375 Hudson Street, New York, NY 10014, U.S.A.
Penguin Group (Canada), 10 Alcorn Avenue, Toronto, Ontario,
Canada M4V 3B2 (a division of Pearson Penguin Canada Inc.)
Penguin Books Ltd, 80 Strand, London WC2R 0RL, England
Penguin Ireland, 25 St. Stephen's Green, Dublin 2, Ireland (a
division of Penguin Books Ltd)
Penguin Group (Australia), 250 Camberwell Road, Camberwell, Victoria 3124,
Australia (a division of Pearson Australia Group Pty Ltd)
Penguin Books India Pvt Ltd, 11 Community Centre, Panchsheel Park,
New Delhi - 110 017, India
Penguin Group (NZ), Cnr Airborne and Rosedale Roads, Albany, Auckland 1310,
New Zealand (a division of Pearson New Zealand Ltd)
Penguin Books (South Africa) (Pty) Ltd, 24 Sturdee Avenue, Rosebank,
Johannesburg 2196, South Africa
Penguin Books Ltd, Registered Offices: 80 Strand, London
WC2R 0RL, England

Designed by Lily Malcom
Text set in Arrus Roman
Printed in the U.S.A. on acid-free paper
10 9 8 7 6 5 4 3 2 1

Library of Congress Cataloging-in-Publication Data
Connor, Leslie, date.
  Dead on town line / by Leslie Connor ; illustrations by Gina Triplett.
      p. cm.
  Summary: A murdered teen's experience of her afterlife
includes her efforts to have her body found and to provide
comfort to her loved ones.
  ISBN 0-8037-3021-7
  [1. Murder—Fiction.] I. Triplett, Gina, ill. II. Title.
  PZ7.C76442De 2005
  [Fic]—dc22
                                                2004015312

To my mother
for her murder mysteries.

To my father
for his images in black and white.

Dead on Town Line

STASH

It was a clever place
To stash the body—
Deep in that crevice
And dead on town line.

Or maybe that was just luck.

The wind ricochets off the
First rise of granite,
Doesn't sweep down,
Doesn't lift up a clue
For the dogs—
Poor dogs.

It's me they're searching for
And I am dead
On town line.

TOWN LINE

The cops have always hesitated to come
All the way out
To town line.
I know because I live there.
Lived there.

We called about
A rabid skunk,
A crazy dirt biker,
A hunter with a gun.

They'd say,
. . . time we get there,
It could cross town line.
Then we can't do anything . . .
. . . not our
Jurisdiction.

But I'm a
Missing Girl,
Not an
Ordinary Nuisance.

ALL-POINTS BULLETIN

I've been simplified
Down to a few details:
Female.   It's true.
Sixteen.   For all of time.
Medium height. Done growing.
Brown hair.   All a-tangle.
Green eyes.   Blank stare.

I'm an All-Points Bulletin
—alerting and alarming—
Both sides of town line.

BODY

From my perch
I'm watching the dogs miss it
Over and over again.
If I could guide them
I would.

The body changes.
This is a cold October.
Rot happens slowly
But it does
Happen.

On request,
The dogs
Seek.
Noses up,
They scan the air—
Find it clean.
Rain-rinsed.

The mat of leaves is deep—
Getting deeper.
The scent is trapped below.
The rains gather
Into rivulets
And carry it away.

GRIDS

Makes sense to check the
Large wooded parcel
Near my home.

Each town is searching for
   . . . the girl with brown hair . . .
Amazing, this turnout—
Both strangers and friends.

And there she is,
Gail Sherman.
She plods through the fallen leaves.
Brings a hand to her brow,
Shelters her eyes from the rain.
She watches the search.
She has to.

Two parties
Of searchers
Walk two different grids.
But they're leaving a gap
That falls wide
On town line.

SEARCHERS

Abel Sorrenson bends,
Eye to the ground,
As if he would
Kiss a
Single blade of autumn grass
For a clue.

(Has Mom remembered
To call him?
Our piano needs tuning.)

No broken twig
Gives up the secret,
No folded needle from
The pine . . .

All good for Gail Sherman.
She rolls her pants legs now—
Damp from these hours
Of sweeping through
October ferns.
She has "sacrificed" her morning.

The searchers say,
Let's move on.
But Abel Sorrenson hangs back.
He scans the grid again.

And Gail Sherman keeps watching.

HUDDLE

The cops huddle
Now and then.
Poker faces and
Low voices,
They scrutinize the players
On the grid.

They say,
No urgency in that stride.
Seem distracted to you?

Been questioned . . .
Seems devastated
Just like all the others . . .

Brother is
Dim as dirt.
Busted him before—
Misdemeanors . . .

No guilt by association . . .

Suppose . . .

Still,
Ask me?
. . . I like that one.

QUESTION

Abel Sorrenson
Shakes the moss off his
Find.

I smell the cold silver,
Feel his question:
Isn't this hers?

He holds two baby spoons
Bent into a circle,
Little handles braided together.
It's a bracelet.
Mine.

Kyle made me that.
It's his spoon.
And my spoon.

Wasn't easy—
Getting it off.
It was always tight
On my wrist.
Thought if I could just leave
Something . . .

(Kyle would've said
I was being
Ridiculously helpful.)

KYLE

Cassie and Kyle.
Kyle and Cassie.
Sounded perfect.
Looked perfect.
And it was
Good.
I could tell him anything—
Almost.

We lay on my bed one afternoon,
Shirts off,
His hand on my belly.
My tears rode a trail
Down my temples to my ears.
Couldn't tell him why—
Didn't know why—
I couldn't do it.
His body felt warm and just right
At my side.

He brought his jacket around me,
Folded me into the cocoon.
He whispered in my ocean ear,
Don't be sad, Cass.
We got time.

SPEARHEAD

Last spring:
I had a Big Idea
For pickers and strummers,
Ticklers and fiddlers—
Anyone hungry for a venue.
And a chance.

This fall:
Composer's Workshop—born!

Abel Sorrenson grinned
When he signed my request
For the old band room by the stage.

He said,
Good to see you
Spearhead
A program like this,
Cassie.
I'll be your advisor.
Can be here in my office—
Working.
But I've got no time to babysit.
This is on
Your shoulders.
Make it work, and I'll write it up—
Nice recommendation for college.

You could use that . . .

Ideas and Leadership—
Name of the game . . .

Any shenanigans,
And it's over.

SWISH

Through the late afternoons in early fall
We played
Echoes of everything
From Bach to Rock.
We lifted our feet—
Syncopated swish—
For the custodian with his mop.
We had some stops and starts
But mostly
We had
Harmony.

Till Gail.

SHOES

Mom always said it:

Walk all the way around
Each person that you meet—
Spend a little time in
Their shoes.

At school they ask it,
Drum it in,
Demand it:

Be kind to others.
Be compassionate.
Be a friend.

And so I tried.

GAIL

Gail Sherman walked up
From out of the blue
And asked to be my friend.
She stood on my toe
Smelled like wet wool
And kept staring at Kyle.
She asked me about Composer's Workshop.

Be kind to others.
Be compassionate.

I told Gail
The workshop is open to
Everyone.

DOG BITE

Death's hard to explain.
Even now,
When I should know.
It reminds me of
A dog bite . . .

A collie got me—
Years ago—
When I was crossing a field.
Came without warning.
I winced at the
Punctures,
Was amazed by
The bruising—
Deeper by the hour.

I was almost relieved
To find out:

Okay,
So this is a
Dog bite.

And okay,
So this is
Death.

But like the bruising,
More seems to be coming.
Being dead
Isn't being done.

POWERS

I've got something . . .
Energy—
Maybe even power.
It is
Like praying, but I can't merely ask.
Like wishing, but I can't just pine.
It's like the wanting I once did
With my old earthly heart.

ANOTHER

I knew she was here.

She kept going by me.
Branch-walking, I call it.
I learned to do it—
Just stepped out—
Had nothing to lose.
Can't drop to my death.

She's dead too.
She switches
From film to threads,
From whiteness to gel,
And sometimes she shimmers
Like stars on obsidian.

She's like me:
Roughly the shape of a girl—
No fingertips.

She flaps a ghost hand at me
Now and then.
Not like
Hello—

More like
Keep out
Of
My
Way.

She's how I found out that
We ghosts can affect
Some earthly matter:
The branches bend.
The leaves rustle.

And I always thought
That was just the wind.

PEST

I say,
Excuse me, do you know
What to do?
Is there anything *to* do?
What's next?

Silence.

I say,
Come on now!
Tell me something!

Silence.

Suddenly, she speaks
Like I've made her spit it up.
She says,
Shoot!
You a pest!

BIRDIE

She tells me,
All's I know is
The ones that ain't ready to go
Stays here.
The ones what hasn't
Been found.
Like me . . .

. . . an' now you.

Well,
Ain't nobody to care 'bout me.
I'm Birdie.
I'm jus' a missin' chicken,
Penny down a drain.

WAS

Birdie says,
Diff'rent fo' you.
Somebody wanna find you real bad.
So many folks.
And them dogs.
Feel the hunt?
All night an' now day.
When it was me,
Nobody looked.

I say,
No one? Never?

Birdie says,
So long ago anyways.
Ain't nobody left t' know my name.
So what they call you?

I look at my ghost hands.
Fingers melt away.
I have no edges.

I tell Birdie,
Well,
Once I was
Cassie Devlin.

OTHERS

Birdie has seen others come and go.

Where?
I want to know.

She says,
Dunno.
Ain't been to the next.
Only been here.
I ain't been found.
Told you that.

I ask Birdie,
Is that what I feel?
The next?
Is that what tugs?

(It's like waiting for a musical note
To be played.)

I tell Birdie,
Feels like I belong there . . .
But I don't know how to go.

Birdie nods,
Says,
Same fo' me.

PEER

Birdie and I peer down into the crevice,
Can see right through
Those October leaves.

She says,
Funny
'bout you an' me—
Bein' kil't
So nears t' the same spot.

I say,
Were we?

She says,
Uh-huh.
I'm jus' down there—
Jus' down the hill.

(She waves a ghost hand.)

Says,
Could see this crack in the rocks
From the house—

Wuz a house . . .
Long time ago.

Anyways,
Use t' snitch a smoke,
Come out here
An' be by my ownself.

Wuz a pretty nice spot—
This ol' crack in the rocks.

MINE

Birdie and I look at my body.
She says,
Well, ain't you all well-fed
An' pretty?

I say,
Not so pretty
Anymore.

I'd wipe the blood from the nose if I could
But that is not a ghost trick,
Or not one I know.
Almost black now,
The blood is like paste
From nose to mouth.
It fills the crack,
Seals the lips.

It's all below
October leaves
Waiting for my
Living Ones—
Poor Living Ones.

PIANO

Mom taught me
　　To play it
　　　　. . . my fingers press the weighted keys,
　　　　　　each hammer finds its wire . . .
　　Helped me to love it
　　　　. . . vibrations have the voices of
　　　　　　quaking earth and falling snow . . .

Mom never loved my fusion
But she was careful
With my spirit.
In return
I carried her Chopin
All up and down my backbone—
Little reminder,
Little resistance.

(I was just learning to be grateful for our struggle.)

We both write music.
Wrote music.
Now she can't.
I can't.

. . . and there's a new piece
right there in my pocket . . .
. . . a piece I'll never finish.

SPLIT

Birdie asks about
My split head.
Hurt much?

I say,
I'd already left the body by then.

She says,
Wanna see
Mine?

HERS

It's buried in the leaf litter
After all these years.

(She thinks it was 1942.)

Hers is all bones
Beside an old stone foundation.
And it's not just hers.
Another's bones lie coiled in her pelvis.

(Reminds me of a squirrel skeleton
I found in the shed once.)

She says,
The man—
He wuz a bad 'un,
An' a lazy dawg.
Din't dig the hole so deep—
Jus' 'nuff t' keep me hid.
He take his mornin' piss
On that patch ev'ry day
Just t' keep the critters off—
Keep 'em from diggin' me up.

I look at the bones of Birdie's unborn—
Pretty far along.

DIMES

Birdie says,
He be nice at first.
He bring me up from Virginia
Being all church-man-like.
He start to preachin'—
Make it up as he go.
He gits folks fooled,
They fill his basket
Full o' dimes on Sundays.

He tells folks he take me in for to
Save my soul.
He tell me he *own* my mulatto ass
And he poke it if he want to
For a dime a week
An' a roof ovah my head.
He got some
Big pawin' hands
An' heavy as a rain barrel,
He wuz.
After a while,
I jus' tell myself it ain't really me
Stuck 'neath him like that.

    I be weedin' the garden,
    I be warmin' the coffee,
    I be hangin' up the wash in the sun . . .

I take them dimes
Put 'em under the plank
Till I got somewheres else to go.

BABY

I ask Birdie
Where her baby is now
Even if it is a ghost baby.

She says,
Dunno.
I seen her go
Quick—
Little firefly—
Through the woods
Right soon as he
Put us in the hole.
Maybe she in the next
Or
Somewheres better.

Miss that wigglin'
She used to do—
My little wigglin' baby.

QUIVER

I throw my ghost at a
Single yellow leaf.
Try to
Blow it,
Lift it,
Move it
Somehow.
All I get is a little quiver—
Damn thing.

Birdie says,
Poo!
That leaf ain't goin'
Nowheres.

(But if branches can bend . . .
. . . why not this?)

I wish and will
That leaf to lift.
Hard.
Harder.

I remember music—
The gentle traction of fingertips on ivory keys . . .
The key raises the hammer . . .
The hammer strikes the wire . . .
. . . and then

The leaf
Does
Lift!

Like a fish, it gleams,
Golden in the low sun.
The leaf turns on air,
Then falls to rest
Nestled in a single, perfect
Depression in the mud.

PRINT

From up in the branches
The boot print is
Clear.

I ask Birdie,
Can you see it?

She shrugs.

I say,
It comes up at me
Like I'm falling toward it.
I smell it.
Feel it all over.

Birdie says,
That's how you know
You dead!

Abel Sorrenson kneels,
Picks the single yellow leaf
From the ground.

He draws his fingertips across the soft mud,
Traces a single, perfect
Depression in the earth.

TALK

The searchers can't get over my
Bracelet.
And now the
Boot print too.
They are flooding the ground with
Beams of light,
Photographing,
Taking a mold,
Checking make and model.

The searchers say,

The boyfriend
Is the one who says
She likes walking in
The woods.
Says she goes off on her own
Sometimes.
Think we should
Talk to him again?

LAST

I tell Birdie,
Oh!
Kyle should not have been
The last to see me.

(Last known.)

He should not have come
Searching these woods
On his own.
He should not have left
That print to
Haunt me—
I'm the ghost!

Birdie says,
He don't know
Wha's like fo' you.
Can't.

I try to wipe the print away
But I go through it,

Or,
It goes through me.

Birdie says,
Leave it 'lone now,
Cassie Devlin.
You ain't doin'
Nobody
No good.

TUNING

Abel Sorrenson faces two rises of granite.
Arm extended,
He turns,
Checks his site on the grid line.
He plays his way up the invisible wires,
Tuning them.

He should be doing his real job.
But he can't stop searching,
And he can't stop
Trying to tune these wires.

His brows come together—
Familiar face—
Just like
When the stage band falters.
Just like
When the school fails
To cough up a few bucks
For his department.

I feel his question:
Has anyone crossed
This ledge?

A searcher closes a hand on his shoulder,
Tells him,
Come on now, Abel.
Day is gone.
We'll start again tomorrow.

DECLINE

I'm outside
The house on town line.
Through the wide glass doors
I see
Mom.

Abel Sorrenson is there.
He runs his finger
Down the edge of a picture
On the fridge—
One of me,
When I was small.

Mom slips away
When Abel tries to cover her hand with his.

She declines all offers:
The wine,
The tea,
The casseroles,
And she will not speak of the
Recovery—
She says,
Rescue—
Only rescue.

She sits at the piano
But she doesn't play.
She weeps at the keys
I can't hear her crying,
But I can taste those tears.

FRAME

Inside my house there is an empty frame.
Inside the frame there was a picture of me—
Little me—
All dressed up for
My first recital.

(Never told anyone
That I'd peed in my tights that day—
Small secret to the grave.)

The picture stood atop the piano
Until one afternoon . . .
Kyle pulled me up from the bench,
Tucked me against the inward curve of
mahogany.
I arched my back across the piano—
The shining piano.

Such kissing . . .
Slippery kissing . . .

My wrist clipped the picture frame.
The landing shattered the glass.

I said Kyle did it.
Kyle said I did it.
Neither of us could stop laughing.

Later, I took the frame apart.
Balanced it back on the piano—
No back, no front, no picture of me.

I told Kyle,
It's modern art—
A square
Of air.

MORNING MUSIC

So often
My music called in the mornings
And I tiptoed,
Closed my mother's door,
Gently.
Didn't want to disturb her . . .
. . . didn't want her to disturb me.

Just past sunrise
I looked up from my practice,
Peered through the square—
Through the empty picture frame.

Out beyond our wide glass doors
Daylight was growing
In the yard,
Confined,
Highlighted
By the border of the frame.

For many mornings
I played what I saw
Within the square—

Just that small serving of the day:
The hop of a bird,
The fall of the rain,
The springing back of a leaf—
Droplets riding on air . . .

My fingers barely left the keys,
My eyes never left the view.
I played the
Silences,
I played the
Singing notes . . .

How I loved my morning music.

MOTHS

I tried, tried, tried
To put my morning music
To the page
But it always left me too soon.

Then once
In the still-dark
The moths danced
At our wide glass door.
I watched them through the
Empty frame.

At the lamp,
They fluttered and bumped,
Receded,
But did not leave;
Kept coming back for more.
I played their refrains till I had them
Like a habit
And finally,
I began to scribble down the notes—
The Morning of the Moths—
My music.

IMPOSSIBLE

The first time Gail Sherman came
To Composer's Workshop
We gave her the stage.

The second time,
She took it
And she never gave it back.

She played an impossible violin—
Bowed a perfect lick,
A singing melody,
Then scorched it
With angry improv.

Okay.
So it's a workshop.
I thought
Gail might find patience,
Grow a little . . .
Somehow.

But every week she came back
Singeing her strings,
Shredding her bow,
And leaving no limelight for anyone else.

The Gail Sherman Show
Wore a hole in us
That I wasn't sure we could
Crawl out of.

Everyone told me,
You're in charge.
You have to do it.
Take that girl out to the woodshed, Cassie.

LEAF-FALL

I listened to her steps
Closing in on my steps.
We walked out of the school
And into the first
Leaf-fall.

Gail wanted to know
    What did I think
        What did I think
            What did I think
                Of her playing?

I told Gail,
You have good energy
And enthusiasm . . .
. . . and . . .
. . . talent.

I told myself,
You are *spineless,* Cassie Devlin!
This girl is *ruining* the workshop.

. . . and Abel Sorrenson,
        shut behind his door,
        isn't going to want to hear
        anything about it.

ENDLESS

Gail on my mind
Morning,
Noon,
Night.

Went to see her
At her house—
More of her music.
Not all good,
Not all bad,
But endless . . .
. . . and I was restless,
    itching for home
    and my own piano keys.

What to tell her?
How to tell her?
I tried.

Said,
My mother encourages me
To slow my practice.
To listen better,
And to hear the silences.

So I imagine
. . . that I am playing on the strings
        inside the piano,
. . . that I am listening through the skin
        on my fingertips.

And any harshness I feel
Melts away.
My music becomes full.

I asked Gail,
Does that make sense to you?

RIDE

Gail said,
Makes me crazy to play
So slow!
Must make you nuts—
Having your mother ride your ass
All the time.
You should get
My deal, Cassie:
My mother's music is
Ice in a glass.
She comes through the door,
Makes a little
Sleepy-gal cocktail—
Fistful of pills,
Shot of booze
On the rocks—
She goes down for the count.
Never bothers me.

I sucked a breath
While Gail played
Another chaotic pass.

JUMP

Gail's twin brother, Jory, came in,
Sat with us for hours,
Not speaking.

Didn't seem like the sharpest
Pencil in the box—
He followed Gail around like a dog.
If she said jump,
Jory jumped—
Sky high.

THOUGHT

Gail said,
Jory's no good
At anything.
Right, Jor-boy?

He just smiled,
Nodded.

Gail cackled like a bird,
Said,
Tried being smart,
Tried for good grades.
But that didn't work—
Did it?

Jory snickered,
Nodded,
Said,
Nope.

I said,
Schoolwork isn't
The only thing that matters.

You have to figure out
What you really love.
Anyone can do that.

And I saw Jory Sherman
Lose his grin
In a thought.

HEADS-UP

I gave Gail
A heads-up.
Told her,
Hey,
The workshop has to be about
Everybody.
You've got to
Let everyone play and
Be heard.

Gail said,
So, they're all
Mad at me?
Talking bad about me?

I said,
They just want their
Fair share.
There's so little time.
Everyone wants to play
Their music.

She said,
No,
It's me.
They don't like me.
They would never
Do this to you.

SESSION

Gail turned up at my house,
Tapped on the glass,
Violin case in her hand.

She said,
Hey!
We should play a session
Together.

While she rosined her bow
I folded my score—
Tried to hide
That I wasn't happy to see her.

All afternoon
I fought, fought, fought
To hold her to a rhythm.
Said a little prayer
That she might
Catch it.

But Gail played on
Furiously
And my piano seemed to shrink
Under my fingertips.

The afternoon wore away.

NEW

Kyle asked what I had in my hand,
And feeling like a shining star
I said,
I wrote something new
For the piano.

He said,
Looks old.

I said,
I keep erasing. . . .

Eyes smiling,
He reached and read,
Said,
Morning of the Moths?
Play for me!

But I clutched the
Worn-thin
Score in my hand—
My precious, penciled
Piece of music.

I told Kyle,
Can't play it for you yet!
I need more time . . .

 63

. . . but you'll be the first to hear . . .

I promise.

CHANCE

I tell Birdie
I was here before—
At this foundation,
Your foundation.
Kyle and I sat on this wall.
He wrapped his legs round my middle,
Pulled me closer.
He pressed a kiss
Into the crease of my neck
And just about melted me into these
Old, crumbly stones.

How I miss him now . . .
. . . miss him miss him miss him . . .

He wanted to know what it was
About Gail Sherman—
Why I stuck by her
Like I did.

(He said she gave him the creeps
From Day One.)

I said,
Maybe a loser is only a loser
Because everyone else thinks so.

She's got some talent,
Have to give her a chance.
You never know—
There might be good
Inside of Gail.

He said,
Don't think so . . .
But guess that's why
I love you.

LIE

Gail stole
One of my sweaters,
Some of my jewelry.
Told people we were
Musical partners.

She said,
Keep it a secret.
Cassie doesn't want everyone to know yet.

When that lie caught her,
She cried.
She said,
I just wanted to be like you,
Cassie.
Someday I
Will
Be like you.

LIKE

I told Gail,
Hey, don't get upset.
Think I don't have bad days
Just like everyone else?

Sure I do.

You don't have to
Be like me, Gail.
Just be your best—
Be you.

UNTIL

I hung in there
Until . . .
Gail said
Kyle touched her.
(He would never!)

Until . . .
I walked into the workshop
And heard
Gail Sherman
Butchering
The Morning of the Moths—

My music!

BOILING

Damn, damn, damn her—
Damn that girl!

I held back—
(Had to.)

Forced a nod and a smile
At Abel Sorrenson
As he passed through the band room.

(Couldn't let him see me boiling.)

When had Gail snagged my score?

Had to have been
Right off
My music stand,
Right in
My own house.

I waited for the click of Abel's office door.

Stopped the music
And
Faced Gail Sherman.

CRESCENDO

Slammed my hands
On a desktop—BAM!

. . . a dozen ashen faces stared . . .
. . . Composer's Workshop, frozen . . .

Told Gail,

Enough!

Said,
That's my melody line!
My music!

Gail tilted her head.
Said,
Cassie,
We worked on this
Together.
Remember . . .
Our sessions at your house?
How else would I
Know the piece by heart?

I said,
Liar!
You stole it!
That's *my* work.

That piece is for
Piano,
Gail.
It isn't even done!
Can't
You
Hear that?

SWALLOW

I pulled Gail into the hall,
Said,
Think I'll roll over
For you
Again,
Gail?

I won't!

You messed with
My stuff,
My boyfriend,
My music!
My—everything!

No place for a thief
In this workshop, Gail.
If you try to come back
I'll tell Mr. Sorrenson
Everything
You've done.

I took a hard swallow.

Said,
I want that score back.
Now.
It's mine!

Her lips barely moved.
She whispered,
It's at my house—
You can just
Go get it.

AFTERMATH

Gail marched away
And left my knees
Shaking.

I went back into the workshop—
Whispering workshop.

Couldn't talk to anybody.

Ran the replay
In the aftermath—
Gail so cool,
So even.
Like ice.

I dropped into a chair,
Put my head on my arms
And waited
For the afternoon
To end.

BETWEEN

Kyle's eyes were
Pinking up
When he met me in the hall.

He said,
Gail told me
You want us to
Take a break.

I buried my face in his chest—
. . . *tired . . . tired . . . tired.*

I said,
And you believe her?
What's Gail Sherman
Between you and me?

He said,
I'm asking you,
Cass.

I said,
We're fine! I promise!
. . . *long, long horrible day . . .*
We'll talk tonight.
I'm sorry,
Have to go.
Have to get my music.

He said,
What music? Where?

Come back!

Cassie!

Hey, Cassie!

FOOL

Birdie says,
You a fool,
Cassie Devlin.
You git your music
But wha' for?
Now you jus' dead!

I say,
Couldn't let it go.
It was
My music.
Mine.

SPY

I am inside the house
On town line—
My house.
Mom's house.

(Wasn't sure I could do this.
Some things are easy.
Some not.)

Mom is at the piano again.
Not playing. Just sitting.
I'm like a spy.
I'm trying to touch her
But I can only pass through.
Her hair riffles,
Falls against her cheek.

Is that me?

FAMILY

I tell Birdie
We were a small family,
Mom and me.
It's hard knowing that
I was her
Everything.
Wish I could tell her
She taught me right.
I knew how to stay away from danger.
Wish I could tell her
This isn't
Her fault.

LOVE

Birdie says,
Din't know
Somethin' bad
Could happen t'
Somebody
What got love
Like you got.

I say,
Guess love cannot protect—
Not completely.
Still,
Love is good.

STORM

The searchers say . . .

*. . . boyfriend's boot print was
Too fresh in the mud,
Not deep enough to have been
More than his own weight—
Couldn't have been carrying a girl
At the time.*

*Doesn't mean
He doesn't know
Something . . .*

I bounce the branches,
Set the clingy leaves
Rattling.

Abel Sorrenson looks up.
Says,
. . . storm warning . . .

WAVE

I tell Birdie,
Watch this!

I slide my ghost hand under
One tulip tree leaf.
Wish it
This way,
That way,
Wish a wave at Birdie.

She says,
Yeah,
But what anybody care
'bout a waving leaf?

SHIVERS

I find Kyle
Sitting on his porch
In the cold October air.
I ghost through him,
Try to warm him.
He shivers.

Oh, my Skinny Boy . . .
If you don't eat again soon
Your pants will slip down . . .

I sweep scarlet leaves
Into a pile at his feet.
I try for a heart shape
But the edges are crooked
And then
More leaves fall.

He'll have a
Next October.
And who might love
My Skinny Boy by then?

Will she be anything
Like me?

RIGHT

I go back to Birdie,
Tell her
She is right:
I am a fool.
A dead
Fool.

Birdie says,
Well,
You ain't the only one.

CAKE

Birdie tells me,
Preacher man bring me a cake that day.
Sweet little pink cake
All fo' me.
He watch me eat it.
He say the baby be okay with him.
I can keep it.
I know I got all them dimes.
Gonna run from him anyways.
I eat every crumb
Of that cake.

Din't know poison
Be so sweet.

My baby,
She slow down inside.
Then I be slow too . . .
So slow I can't run.

He bury us down—
Little hole b'side the house
Like you seen.
It all burn down now anyways—
With my dimes.

HIM

I ask Birdie,
Is that preacher
Dead yet?

She says,
Yeah, he dead.
But first he get real old—
Shrunk-up pecker.
And he have a bad time of it.

Birdie's threads hum.

When he die,
He don't come through here.
Not this way.

I coulda stuffed him a chicken
Full of ground glass,
Give him poison,
Done same what he did.
I coulda kil't
Him
For the baby.

VIAL

I tell Birdie,
Mine was poison too—
A drug.
It started like that, anyway.

I went to get
My music.

But it was just Jory
At the house.
He gave me my score,
Watched me tuck it in my pocket.

He said,
Hey, Cassie,
You like getting high?

I saw the vial in his thick fingers.

I said,
No, Jory.
Put that away.
I turned to leave.

He grabbed my wrist
And stood still as a tree.

He said,
You have to.
Gail said so.

I tried to twist out of his grip—
Kicked,
Screamed.
He told me,
Quit it, Cassie!
Huge punch in the face—
And I fell.

FADE

Jory put his knee on my chest,
Pulled my lip open.
The bitter taste seeped in.
He held my jaw,
Counted.
Said,
Sleepy gal now, Cassie.
Sleepy gal.

Then I faded—
All drunk in my head.

BLACKBIRDS

On my way to dying,
Jory Sherman took me to see
A beautiful thing.

Hey, Cassie.
(He jiggled me awake in the car.)

I opened my eyes,
Made out a field
Full of
Red-winged blackbirds
On straw-colored stalks.

. . . *Beautiful.*

Jory said,
It's getting cold.
They'll be gone soon, Cassie.
I know all about
Those blackbirds.

I slurred,
Told Jory,
I think that stuff
You gave me
Could kill me.
He nodded,
And the blurry birds bobbed.

 93

HILL

He took me right past the end
Of my own driveway.
I looked up the first hill.
Couldn't see the house.
Couldn't say
Good-bye.

SLAMMING

In the woods
Jory moaned,
Jesus, Gail!
What are we gonna do?
She won't die!

(I took a lot of slamming.)

Gail,
Up on the ledge,
Laughed and cried all at the same time.
Told him,
That's right, Jory!
Throw her down again!

HOLE

The drug worked—
Deadened every blow.
I felt Jory Sherman drag me up.

(Tried to dig my nails into his doughy arm.)

Told him,
Don't . . .
    Do . . .
        This . . .

Sick sound—
My rib
Bursting through my lung.
The heat of a thousand needles
Seared through me.

Cold leaves on my cheek
Made me open my eyes . . .
One last time.

I saw Jory's muddy sock—
Anklebone poking
Through a hole.

Then nothing.

OUTSIDE

From outside—
From away
I watched
Jory tug that body up again.
He threw it down
One last time—
Split my head on a rock.

Jory beat his fists
On the ground
And hollered,
Why, Gail? Why?

Then Jory Sherman
Curled up and cried.

VESSEL

I threw my brand-new ghost
At that body—
My body.
Wanted to

GET

BACK

IN.

Wanted to slide my soul
Back down into those fingertips.
But it was all closed up—
My vessel,
My wreck.

CLARITY

Now,
Free from the confines of
Flesh and Bone
There is a clarity.
It dawns the same way
My music once did—
In sequences and silences,
Parts moving together.
I can hear what's inside of Gail
And it makes sense too.
It was all about her.
Never me.

(My death—so unimportant.)

She sees these
Spaces
Open now:

Bright Musician.
Student Leader.
Admired Friend.

Spaces
Gail created.

Spaces
Gail intends to fill.

 99

WHISTLE

The leaves
Swish-whistle
When I raise them,
Send them cartwheeling
On still air.

I get them going
A few at a time now—
Lento.
Allegro!

Birdie throws her ghost at a sycamore leaf.
She says,
Poo!
Ain't goin' nowheres.

I say,
Don't force it up—
Let it up.
Think of the branches, Birdie . . .

And then Birdie does it—
Lifts her leaf!
Has it making loops in the air.
First slow.
Now faster!

TOUCH

I reach for Birdie,
For her edgeless fingers—
And—
Zap!
She sails back
Like a bedsheet in a storm.
Branches snap and fall.
She reassembles . . .
Slowly.

I ask Birdie,
You all right?
Does it hurt?

She steams,
Says,
No, it don't hurt!
I'm dead—pest!

I say,
That was power!

That was
Touch!

CHURN

I beg Birdie,
Please try to be with me.
And I'll try to be with you.

We are circling—
I'm catching up to Birdie.
Birdie's catching up to me.

She lets me float in.
I let her float in.
Like swimmers,
We glide!

Our threads pulse.

The key lifts the hammer,
The hammer strikes the wire . . .

I say,
Play it with me, Birdie!

The branch sways—
    A bow to the string.
Songbirds scatter—
    The sweep of chimes.
We churn the leaves
With our tipless toes.
Fast, faster!

Birdie says,
Sheee-it!
You Cassie Devlin, you!
What in hell is this?

I say,

Music!

ORCHESTRATING

Abel Sorrenson
Is pissing mad.

He asks,
What is town line?
It's invisible! Imaginary!
Something that belongs
To both sides
And
To neither!

He spreads a map of two towns
Across the old stone foundation,
Catches his breath,
Begs everyone to
Look and listen.

He says,
We have failed to search
Across town line.
We've stopped just short
Again and again.

He shows them
The grids,
Extends the lines—
With red pen.

Says,
It's not much in acreage,
But what if she's there?

CLEARANCE

Seems there were papers to be signed
By each side of town line.

Looks like
Clearance
Has been
Granted.

The searchers
Take broad strides,
Refreshed
By morning light
And new prospects.

They walk the grids,
Weave their pattern
Over uncovered spaces.

Closer now,
Closer now . . .

. . . they're stitching the gap.

CHEAT

Gail Sherman
Rejoins the party
Pretends to search.
Jory lumbers behind her,
Steps on her heel.
She glares.

Both of them
Cheat at this game on the grid—
Came with the answers
Already in hand.

I bring a maple leaf down slowly,
Let it hover,
Then bother
One Sherman
And the other.

Gail bats at my leaf,
Forges ahead . . .
. . . *a hero in the making?*

Jory swats his own ear
And sweats
In the cold sun.

STRUM

Birdie and I
Strum the black and yellow tape
Till it rattles and whines.
Jory turns
A nervous eye toward the sound.
Gail socks him in the arm.

I tell Birdie,
I don't think I could have
Loaded him with drugs,
Split his head,
Even if I had known
He'd do that to me.

She says,
I coulda!
Lemme at him!

I say,
But he's the weak one.
A pawn.

(. . . and I've got bits of
his skin
beneath my dead-girl nails . . .)

RIFT

The searchers are
Standing atop
The crevice rocks—

Right there.

They talk,
They drone,
Knock mud from their treads.
But they don't reach into the rift,
Don't disturb
The sodden sponge of leaves.

ECHO

I say,
Hey, Birdie,
Think we
Could move my leaves?

She says,
All them leaves?
Dunno.
Maybe if it's jus'
One leaf at a time—

I echo Birdie,
I say,

. . . one leaf at a time . . .

. . . one leaf at a time . . .

SNAP

My threads hum.

Can I be found?
Can I do it?
Should I do it?

Might be Justice.
And
Peace of mind
For my Living Ones—
Loving Living Ones.

Once more
The light dies from the sky.
Searchers leave.

I pound across the branches—
Snap-crack one clean off.

It doesn't seem right
That there is anything
I still need to do.
I'm dead!

But I'm not done.

ONE

It takes just one
Relentless
Leaf
Scraping across the cold cement floor
Of a porch with torn screens
At the Sherman house.

The leaf follows Jory,
Puts his back
Into a corner.
It curls in on itself,
Turns end over end
Then opens flat again.

Jory—
On his toes,
Breathes hard,
Fast.
He blinks
In the twisted darkness . . .

. . . the leaf inches forward . . .

Jory bolts.
Slams
Into a post,
Bloodies his face.

FOUND

Jory Sherman
Breaks.

He leads the searchers
To the crevice.

They begin to carry off my leaves—
Handfuls of leaves—
So gently.

Abel Sorrenson cannot watch
Now that he knows
I will be found.
He stoops,
Drops his arm around
One of the dogs,
Puts his forehead into the ruff.

The dog whines and whimpers . . .

. . . and so does Jory Sherman,
All covered in snot.

Wonder if his
Blackbirds
Have all gone . . .

MAD CAT

Gail scrambles up the hill
To the crevice,
To the searchers,
To Jory.
She screeches at him—
Says:
What did you do?
What the hell did you do?

He stares back—no expression . . .

Gail swipes at the ground
Brings up a rock
And flings it—
Gashes Jory's brow.

They struggle to pin her.
Mad cat
In a trap—
She thrashes.

Gail Sherman—
So impossible to hold.

 115

LIFT

They lift the body—
My body—
From the cradle of the crevice.

They tuck my hands,
My curled fingers
Neatly across my chest—
And all as if
I am a treasure,
More precious now
Than when I lived.

    This is a second parting:
    I left the body
    Now the body leaves me.
    That shape—
    The flesh-and-bone girl,
    My host for sixteen years—
    Has a new purpose now:
    She is a vessel for my story;
    A ship of evidence.

My ghost
Glows
Like new song.

I tell Birdie,

I am found!

RIPPLE

My threads hum,
Ripple
With a current,
Then surge like a spark
That never stops firing.

Birdie catches the buzz,
Says,
Lookie here!
(She trembles.)
An' I ain't even tryin'!

The searchers are leaving.
Abel Sorrenson
Heads back toward the old foundation—
Birdie's foundation.

I need
    One
        more
            thing
Before I can let him go.

I fix Birdie
With a fiery light,
Tell her,
Come with me!

She says,
Wha' for?

I say,
Hurry!

SWEEP

We link up,
Start the churning,
Build the pulse.
We sweep down on the old foundation
Spread the leaf litter,
Ancient ashes
And blackened dimes.
We pour our ghosts over Birdie's bones,
Blow the layers
And the years
Away from her grave.

OUT

On the way out,
Abel Sorrenson walks beside
The old foundation,
Puts a foot
Down the hole,
Down on Birdie's bones.

He drops to his knees,
Scrabbles in the humus,
Pushes at the dirt and leaves
With his hands.

He cries,
There is
Something here!
Someone!
And—little bones
Oh my God!
Little baby bones!

Slowly he draws his fingers over
The remains,
So long nestled
In the ground.

Birdie and I hover
In the branches
As they carry us
Out of
The silent woods.

FALLING

I ask Birdie,
Do we go now?
And where?

She says,
Dunno.
Never been nowheres else . . .

. . . keep tellin' you that . . .

But somethin's diff'rent . . .
Dunno what . . .

She raises her ghost arms,
Ponders her form.

I watch
The October rain
Falling through Birdie—
Shining Birdie.

FROZEN

Birdie comes spying with me
Inside the house
On town line.

My things sit atop the piano:
Braided bracelet,
Sea-glass earrings,
The folded, worn piano score
From my pocket.

Mom sits, staring at my artifacts.
She seems frozen
Now that I've been found . . .

. . . so near to home.

UNFINISHED

Birdie whisks the folded score
Off the top of the piano.

Mom picks it up from the floor.
She sits on the bench,
Smooths the pages on the stand.
She curls her fingers above the keys,
Pauses,
Then begins.
She plays,
Cries.
She slows when she sees
That my work is
Unfinished.

GRACE NOTES

Birdie says,
You could give her the rest,
Cassie Devlin.

I say,
She knows.
   She must
        After all those mornings—
        Notes heard
        In her sleep . . .

The silence tugs.

Birdie links her gel to mine,
Starts the pulse.
I pour forward
With the grace notes
And find my way
To my mother's aching heart.

FINGERTIPS

Her fingertips—
Beautiful fingertips—
Find the keys again.
My mother plays.

High and light
The notes climb—
Refrain of tremolos and trills.
She plays
The echoes of
Ever-beating,
Ever-working wings.

Slow and low,
Restful dips
Supply breath.
The melody emerges,
Pours out like colors.

It is sorrow casting off its weight,
The moths dancing
Into morning.

My work,
My joy—
Set free—
In my mother's hands.

 127

Music!

Mine,
And
Hers.

WHEEL

Kyle hears piano-song.
Lets himself into my mother's house.

He stands beside her—
Listening.

He fingers the bracelet,
Tips it up like a wheel.
Rolls it
This way,
That way.
His eyes close.
He whispers,

. . . Cassie.

HOVERING

I am hovering in the peak,
Lingering
Close to
Mom and Kyle,
These two hearts—
Poor wounded hearts—
The two
I love
The most.

This is a cold October . . .

. . . and I will soon be leaving.

CODA

Birdie floats.
Her threads are calm.
I am surging away from her.
Unplanned.
Unworried.
I call to her,
Will I see you in the next?

She says,
Dunno . . .
Never been . . .

Her voice sings its own
Harmony—

Something pulls me . . .

And I am gone.

ACKNOWLEDGEMENTS

With thanks to these very helpful pre-publication readers:

Nancy Antle, Doe Boyle & Caitlin, Erin, Devan & Laura Boyle, Martha Bradshaw, Leslie Bulion, Mary-Kelly Busch, Jonathan Connor, Marley Connor, Sam Connor, Ian Connor, Kate Duke, Mary J. Elliott, Nancy W. Hall, Lorraine Jay, Kay Kudlinski, Sandi Shelton & Stephanie Shelton, Sanna Stanley, Judy Theise, Nancy Elizabeth Wallace, and the members of the SCBWI Shoreline chapter.

For their help with the music, I thank Marilynn Buehler and Mac Petrequin, as well as Chris Taylor and Richard Milgram.

For sharing their stories about search and rescue dogs and their handlers, I thank Joanne and Hod Wilcox and their beautiful dog, Talon.

For helping me find the whole story, I thank Jennie Dunham and Cecile Goyette.